MICK ELLIOTT

SQUIDGE DIBLEY

DESTROYS HISTORY

LOTHIAN
Children's Books

FOR LOU

A Lothian Children's Book
Published in Australia and New Zealand in 2019
by Hachette Australia
Level 17, 207 Kent Street, Sydney NSW 2000
www.hachettechildrens.com.au

Text and illustration copyright © Mick Elliott 2019

 A catalogue record for this
book is available from the
National Library of Australia

ISBN 978 0 7344 1969 9

Cover design by Christa Moffitt, Christabella Designs
Cover illustration by Mick Elliott
Series text design by Amy Daoud
Internal design for this edition by Christa Moffitt, Christabella Designs
Author photograph courtesy of Melissa Mai
Printed and bound in Australia by McPherson's Printing Group

CHAPTER 1

The whole DISASTER started when Ms Trigley gave us a history assignment.

This is MS TRIGLEY.

This is us.

CRAGLANDS SOUTH PRIMARY

CLASS 6PU

PADMAN O'DONNELL

• Best friend of Squidge Dibley.
• Writer. Cartoonist in training.
• Narrator and illustrator of this story! (Yes, that's me!)

SQUIDGE DIBLEY

- Newest student at Craglands South Primary.
- Best friend of Padman 'Pod' O'Donnell.
- Genius inventor.
- Special, stretchy medical conditions.* (See page 20)

LEANNA KINGSLEY

- Science nut. Space fanatic.
- Claims to spot U.F.O.s almost every day.

THE PRITCHARD TWINS (AINSLEY & AUDREY)

- Identical twins, no-one is ever sure who is who.
- Pranksters since preschool.

4

DANIEL KWON-YOON

- Skateboard fanatic.
- Dream in life: to win an Olympic gold medal for skateboarding.

RENNIE GROSE

- Obsessed with pythons. Keeps one as a pet, but may have hundreds more.

REBECCA PETERSON

- Musical genius. Plays every instrument in the Craglands South Primary orchestra (sometimes all at once).

ABIGAIL TAKANI

- Sugar sachet collector.
- Junior champion street dancer.

SHANE SLOOSMAN
• Eternally nervous friend of Lenny Battisto.

LENNY BATTISTO
• Not *as* nervous but still *pretty* nervous friend of Shane Sloosman.

NATHAN KOBEISSI
• Cannot stop eating paint. If there is paint available, Nathan will find it. And eat it.

CRICHTON PEEL
• Most annoying kid on planet earth. And probably in the universe.

So that's us. And *THIS* was the history assignment Ms Trigley gave us:

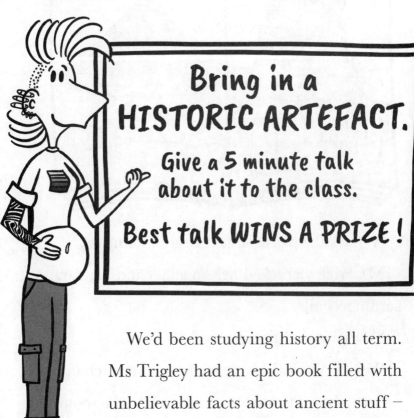

Bring in a
HISTORIC ARTEFACT.
Give a 5 minute talk
about it to the class.
Best talk WINS A PRIZE!

We'd been studying history all term. Ms Trigley had an epic book filled with unbelievable facts about ancient stuff – like how the pyramids were built entirely by hand.

'What's the prize?' asked Leanna Kingsley.

Ms Trigley cracked her knuckles and blew on her fingernails.

'The prize…' she said.

'Yes…?' we said, leaning forward on our chairs.

'Is…' she said, slowly looking around the room.

'YES?????!' we cried, leaning so far forward that our desks were about to tip over.

Ms Trigley drew in a deep breath and said, 'A genuine, limited edition, mega-jumbo-sized DR DOOGLES GOLDEN CHOCOLATE EGG!'

'WHOA!' we said, collapsing off our seats.

'They only make five of those a year!' said Daniel Kwon-Yoon.

'And only the richest people on earth ever get them,' added Abigail Takani, swallowing a sugar sachet with an excited gulp.

'I've only ever seen one behind bulletproof glass at Dr Doogles' Museum of Priceless Chocolate Delicacies,' said Rebecca Peterson.

'The milk comes from posh cows who eat nothing but pure cocoa beans for their entire lives,' said Leanna Kingsley.

'How did you even get one?' I asked Ms Trigley.

'Good question, Padman,' Ms Trigley replied. 'Just let me say that I have my sources.'

'Wow,' I whispered to Squidge Dibley. 'A genuine, limited edition Dr Doogles mega-jumbo-sized Golden Chocolate egg! I can't even imagine what one would taste like.'

Crichton Peel jumped up on his chair. 'And you'll never find out either,' he shrilled. 'Because I'm going to WIN, losers!'

This was typical, because Crichton is

THE MOST ANNOYING KID IN THE UNIVERSE.

FIVE REASONS WHY CRICHTON PEEL IS THE MOST ANNOYING KID IN THE UNIVERSE

 BRAGS ABOUT BEING SMARTER THAN EVERYONE ELSE. (HE'S NOT.)

 LOVES GETTING OTHER PEOPLE IN TROUBLE. (ALL THE TIME.)

Thinks he's an expert on everything. (He's not.)

 Farts silently in class, then blames the person next to him. (It's always him.)

 Keeps bits of dried snot under his fingernails in case he gets hungry.

Crichton started dancing and chanting,

'That egg is mine.

It's gonna taste fine.

I'm the best.

Forget the rest.

I'm going to smash this history test.

You're gonna lose.

That's your fate.

I'm gonna win that choc-o-late.'

'Ugh!' groaned the Pritchard Twins. 'I can't believe Crichton is already doing a victory dance.'

'You call THAT dancing?' said Abigail Takani.

She leaned back on her chair and said, 'Squidge, drop me a beat.'

Everyone turned to look at Squidge Dibley.

Normally he's pretty quiet, but if there is one thing we have learned since the day Squidge suddenly appeared in the third storey window of our school building, it's that you can count on things to get instantly **FREAKY** when Squidge gets involved.

It may be because Squidge is unlike any other kid at Craglands South Primary.

It may be because Squidge is unlike any other kid on the planet.

It may even be because he is a genius inventor who can build the most awesome creation from a few bits of junk.

But most likely it's because he was born with **BUNGEE BONES, MARSHMALLOW MUSCLES,** a **STRETCHY SKELETON, ELASTIC LEGS** and a whole bunch of **MEDICAL MALADIES** that make his body react in crazy ways to things that happen around him.

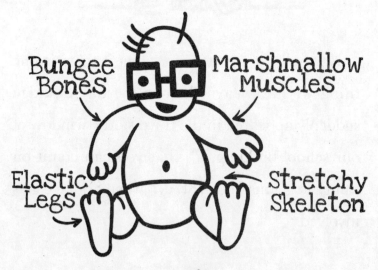

Squidge pressed a button on the side of his desk.

'Never noticed that button before,' I said.

'Special modification,' squeaked Squidge.

His desk began to transform in front of our eyes. The top lifted up on a mechanical arm, then revolved sideways. Two **HUGE** speakers emerged from inside it. Two turntables and a control panel rotated from underneath and clicked into place. A disco ball flew up on a giant pole and the desk was elevated on metal stilts.

Finally, a hatch opened up and a pair of headphones sprung up into the air and landed perfectly on Squidge's head.

'**EPIC!**' said Daniel Kwon-Yoon in awe.

'New invention,' squeaked Squidge, tapping a button. A haze of fog and lasers filled the room.

'DJ DIBLEY IS IN DA HOUSE!' yelled Abigail Takani, ripping open another handful of sugar sachets from her pocket and gulping them down.

Squidge put one hand on his headphones and pressed down on his keyboard.

A noise erupted from the speakers and EXPLODED across the room, blasting Crichton into the wall.

A spotlight hit Abigail Takani and she started popping and locking so fast that she was like a blur.

Abigail is Craglands South Primary's champion street dancer. She is *SO* good that she wins in the senior categories too. She gets all her energy from the endless supply of sugar she keeps in her pockets.

Rebecca Kingsley pulled out her trumpet and started jamming along with Squidge. Within seconds the whole class was transformed into a full-on dance party.

You're probably thinking, why didn't Ms Trigley tell us all to **SIT DOWN** and **GET BACK TO WORK.**

That's because she was too busy having a dance battle with Abigail.

Ms Trigley is the **BEST TEACHER EVER.** She totally gets us, which is the only reason we have learned anything this year.

We used to have this disgusting teacher called Vice Principal Hoovesly.

Luckily, Squidge Dibley came along and destroyed his plans to take over our school.*

[*See *Squidge Dibley Destroys the School*.]

Now, he's the school janitor, but everyone is sure that he is secretly plotting his revenge.

Anyway, Ms Trigley probably would have let the dance battle go all afternoon, but eventually the school principal, Principal Shoutmouth, made a surprise visit to our classroom to make sure that the loud noise wasn't giving Squidge Dibley a nervous reaction.

You see, as well as being my best friend and an unbelievable inventor, Squidge has many special conditions that can go off at any time, especially when there are loud noises.

NERVOUS BELLY BELCHUS

EXPOSURE TO SUDDEN LOUD NOISES SUCH AS SHOUTING, YELLING OR ANGRY OUTBURSTS CAUSE SQUIDGE DIBLEY'S STOMACH TO VIOLENTLY EXPEL A SURGE OF SULPHURIC STOMACH GASES IN THE FORM OF EXPLOSIVE BURPS AND BELCHES.

BUNGEE BONES

IF SQUIDGE GETS BUMPED AT HIGH SPEED, HE LOSES CONTROL OF HIS MOVEMENT AND BOUNCES ERRATICALLY UNTIL GRAVITY SLOWS HIM DOWN.

BLOATUS MAXIMUS

IF SQUIDGE IS FULLY SUBMERGED IN WATER HE ABSORBS ALL LIQUID IN CONTACT WITH HIS BODY. HE EXPANDS

LIKE A MASSIVE SPONGE UNTIL HE IS FIFTY TIMES HIS NORMAL SIZE.

Luckily, Squidge was wearing a special pair of noise-cancelling headphones, so the noise of his sick beats wasn't making him burp. And nobody on the dance floor had bumped into him so he hadn't inflated or caused any catastrophic damage.

But, thanks to the history assignment, it wouldn't be long before he would – on a scale that would change the course of humankind.

CHAPTER 2

For the next week, all anybody talked about was the history assignment. Everyone was **DESPERATE** to win the genuine, limited edition, mega-jumbo-sized Dr Doogles Chocolate egg.

PROPERTY OF
DR. DOOGLES

Or at the very least, just make sure that Crichton **DIDN'T** win it.

Ms Trigley always lets Squidge and I work together on class assignments as a team. Mostly we build inventions in my dad's workshop, using stuff we collect from the junkyard across the road.

We're really into recycling.

Squidge has invented some amazing stuff. Like a remote control scorpion, a trumpet-playing robot and even a massive aquarium maze for Bubble O'Gill the puffer fish, our class mascot.

When I asked Squidge what we should make for the history assignment, he squeaked, 'Let me handle this one, Pod.'

I was happy with that, because with Squidge's

inventing skills I figured we'd be a shoo-in to win the chocolate egg. Plus it meant that I'd have more time to work on the new comic book I was drawing.

CRICHTON PEEL
V
GIGANOTOSAURUS
The Explosive (and STINKY)
TRUE story!

Words and Pictures
by Padman 'Pad' O'Donnell

Looking back, maybe it was a mistake to let Squidge do all the work on our assigment.

Actually, who am I kidding? It was a **MASSIVE** mistake.

But I didn't know that then.

I didn't know **ANYTHING** then.

And if I had known, I'm not sure future me would have believed what was going to happen.

Uh-oh !

FUTURE PADMAN

CHAPTER 3

The day of the history assignment finally came. Everyone had their historic artefacts hidden in boxes. The whole class was buzzing with excitement.

Ms Trigley said that she would draw our names out of a hat to see what order we would speak in.

'Okay, 6PU,' she said. 'I'm looking for juicy historic facts that help us all learn a little bit more about the past. And just a reminder that the best presentation of the day will win the limited edition, mega-jumbo-sized Dr Doogles Chocolate egg.'

She reached into her hat and pulled out a name.

'First up,' she said, looking at the piece of paper. 'We have… Crichton Peel.'

'YEEEESSSSSSS!!!!' screeched Crichton leaping up from his chair. 'BEST GOES FIRST!'

He galloped up to the front of the class hiding a tiny cardboard box in his hand.

'Okay, losers,' he said. 'You are about to see the most AMAZING object ever seen in the history of the world.'

He slowly lifted something out of the little box.

'Check this out!' he said.

It looked like he wasn't holding anything.

We all peered closely. It was impossible to see, especially from where Squidge and I were in the back row.

'What even is that?' whispered the Pritchard Twins.

'This amazing historic object,' said Crichton, 'is over 1.8 million years old.'

'But we can't even see it,' said Daniel Kwon-Yoon.

'It comes from Africa, from the time of the homo erectus,' continued Crichton. 'And it is going to win me that genuine, limited edition, mega-jumbo-sized Dr Doogles Chocolate egg.'

'BUT WHAT ACTUALLY IS IT?!' said Leanna Kingsley.

'This,' said Crichton looking smugly around the classroom, 'is the big toenail of the very first

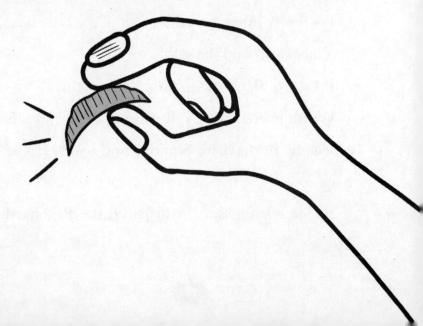

human being who ever walked on earth.'

The whole class was silent for a moment. Then everyone cracked up.

'It's a **TOENAIL?!**' said Abigail Takani, tears of laughter streaming down her face. 'An ancient and mysterious *toenail*?!'

'Dude,' said Daniel Kwon-Yoon. 'It looks like one of *your* toenails. Like, if it's that ancient, shouldn't it at least be fossilised or something?'

'It literally looks like you clipped it off your toe this morning,' said Leanna Kingsley.

Everyone gathered around Crichton trying to get a look at the toenail.

'Show me!' said Shane Sloosman.

'I want to touch the toenail!' said Lenny Battisto.

'Me first!' said Shane Sloosman.

'Hey!' screeched Crichton, jumping up onto a desk. 'Hands off my toenail! It's precious! And historically significant.'

He leapt from desk to desk, as half the class chased him around the room chanting 'TOENAIL! TOE NAIL! HISTORICALLY SIGNIFICANT TOENAIL!'

Suddenly, Crichton tripped. The toenail flew through the air.

It landed in Bubble O'Gill's bowl.

'GULP!' went Bubble O'Gill swallowing the toenail.

'WAAAAAHHHH!' cried Crichton. 'MY PRECIOUS TOENAIL!'

'Never mind, Crichton,' said Abigail Takani. 'You can always grow another one.'

CHAPTER 4

'**T**his ancient glass jar,' whispered Daniel, holding it up, 'has been in my family longer than time itself.'

'It's empty!' scoffed Crichton.

'It may **LOOK** empty,' whispered Daniel, 'but inside is something magical!'

'I'm scared,' said Shane Sloosman.

'You **SHOULD BE SCARED**, Sloosdude,' said Daniel. 'Because the contents of this jar belonged to my ancient ancestor, Jang Seo-Kwon.'

'Ancient ancestor, huh?' chuckled Ms Trigley.

'They're usually the best ones.'

'Jang Seo-Kwon was a simple fisherman,' continued Daniel. 'But also a scientist of the ancient ways.'

'But it's just a dumb, **EMPTY JAR!**' said Crichton, pushing forward to look at the jar close up.

'Please. Have some respect,' said Daniel Kwon-Yoon. 'I am about to demonstrate the powerfully powerful power of the past.'

He placed his hand reverently on the lid and slowly began to unscrew it.

'Prepare to experience...**THE LAST FART OF JANG SEO-KWON!**' 'IT BURNS MY NOSTRILS!!!' cried Crichton, his eyes bulging out of his head.

'Behold the methane of many millennia!' chuckled Daniel.

'That rules!' said the Pritchard twins, breathing it in.

'That reeks!' cried Shane Sloosman.

'That really stinks!' coughed Lenny Battisto.

The vapours rippled across the classroom like a horde of poop-scented ghosts.

'How exactly did your ancestors capture this interesting gas?' asked Ms Trigley opening up the windows.

Daniel shrugged. 'I'm not exactly sure on the specific details,' he said sheepishly.

'I'm also curious,' she added, switching on the ceiling fan, 'why I saw you buying that jar at Kmart yesterday afternoon. I'm pretty sure that you were eating a packet of prunes at the time.'

'History is full of mystery, Ms T,' said Daniel, twisting the lid back on the jar and flopping down on his chair.

'I don't even want to think how he captured that stench,' I whispered to Squidge. But Squidge was busy peering into a big cardboard box under his desk.

Little did we know that when the box was opened, our lives would CHANGE FOREVER.

CHAPTER 5

The chaos continued on a historic scale.

Ms Trigley loved it.

The Pritchard Twins had the first ever sample of joke sneezing powder. They claimed it dated back to Ancient Greek times.

Unfortunately, they spilled it (of course).

Leanna Kingsley claimed to have a piece of the actual meteorite that had DESTROYED the dinosaurs.

Shane Sloosman brought in a pair of hand-carved wooden teeth.

He said that they belonged to his great, great great, great, great, great, great, great grandfather.

Lenny Battisto's artefact was a crumb of caveman snot. It was still STICKY.

Abigail Takani showed us her

collection of vintage sugar sachets. They dated back to 1955.

She let us all try some. Everyone got a little hyper after that.

Rebecca Peterson – who is a total musical genius – played a bone-flute, which was an ancient flute literally carved out of **HUMAN BONE**.

It sounded **SUPER CREEPY**.

'That's because it puts a **DEADLY** curse on anyone who hears it,' explained Rebecca cheerfully plucking a pair of earplugs out of her ears. 'So you're probably all going to suffer **EXCRUCIATING** bad luck from now on.'

She was right.

Squidge was presenting our project next.

CHAPTER 6

As Squidge carried the cardboard box up to the front of the class, nobody could have known what was about to be unleashed.

'Okay, Dibs,' said Ms Trigley. 'I'm expecting **BIG** things.'

Squidge gave her a thumbs-up and carefully placed the box on her desk.

Everyone leant forward on their chairs. The room was whisper-quiet. We figured that we were in for something special. With Squidge, we always got something unexpected.

'For our historic artefact,' squeaked Squidge, carefully removing the tape from the edges of box,

'I need your full attention.'

Crichton rolled his eyes and muttered  under his breath.

'And now,' said Squidge, 'It is time.'

He pulled the tape from the corners of the box. The sides fell outwards, revealing something that looked like…

… well,

… a toilet seat.

It was shiny, metallic and looked like it was made from steel.

'Phhttt,' scoffed Crichton. 'It's just a dumb old dunny seat.'

Ms Trigley studied

Squidge's artefact. 'I'm guessing this is not a regular toilet seat,' she said.

'Not this time,' Squidge giggled.

Ms Trigley tapped on the seat. 'What's it made from?'

'Titanium,' said Squidge proudly.

'Titanium toilet seat, eh? Never heard of one of those before,' said Ms Trigley. 'I get the feeling that you're making history here, Dibs…'

Squidge giggled again and unrolled a power cord from the base of the titanium toilet seat.

'Why does a toilet seat need a power cord?' asked Shane Sloosman nervously.

'Just warming it up,' squeaked Squidge, plugging the cord into the power socket. It started to buzz.

'Electric toilet seat,' chuckled Daniel Kwon-Yoon. 'That'll give you hot, cross buns.'

The buzz from Squidge's titanium toilet seat grew louder.

'I'm SCARED,' whispered Shane Sloosman, cuddling his teddy.

I had no idea what was going to happen next. I started to wonder whether it was a good idea for Squidge to do our assignment solo.

But it was too late now. I was as curious as everyone else to find out what was going to happen next.

Finally it went, DING!

'Ready,' said Squidge with a cheeky smile.

At that moment, an announcement came over the school PA. Principal Shoutmouth's voice echoed across the room.

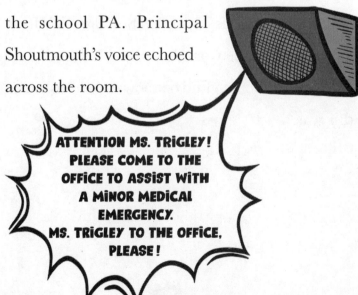

ATTENTION MS. TRIGLEY! PLEASE COME TO THE OFFICE TO ASSIST WITH A MINOR MEDICAL EMERGENCY. MS. TRIGLEY TO THE OFFICE, PLEASE!

As well as being an epic teacher Ms Trigley is a qualified paramedic, so she is always getting called to the office to help with injuries. Apparently she was in the medical branch of the army before she became a teacher.

'Okay, 6PU,' said Ms Trigley. 'Chill for ten and I'll be right back. One of the kindergarten kids probably has their finger stuck up their noise again.'

She told us all to stay put and that we would continue Squidge's presentation as soon as she got back.

'Don't worry, Ms T!' smiled Squidge. 'We have all the time in the world.'

We were about to find out how disastrously true this was.

CHAPTER 7

No sooner had Ms Trigley left the room than the Pritchard twins said, 'What's the matter with Bubble O'Gill?'

We checked out his bowl. He didn't look well.

'What's wrong with him?' said Lenny Battisto.

'He's puffing up!' cried Abigail Takani.

'He's **BLOWING** up,' said the Pritchard twins.

'**HE'S THROWING UP!**' said Shane Sloosman.

At that moment, something burped out of Bubble O'Gill's mouth.

'**MY TOENAIL!**' yelled Crichton Peel. '**MY PRECIOUS TOENAIL! GIVE IT BACK, FISH-FACE!**'

Crichton jumped up and leapt toward Bubble O'Gill's bowl, arm stretched out.

'Crichton! No!' I yelled.

But it was too late. Crichton plunged his hand into the tank, splashing Bubble O'Gill up into the air.

He sailed over our heads like a soccer ball, ricocheted off the ceiling, bounced off Lenny Battisto's head, rebounded off the window, bounced off Shane Sloosman's face and sailed towards Squidge's titanium toilet seat.

'**NOOOOOOOOOOOOOOOOOOO!!!!**' we screamed.

But our screaming made Squidge **BUUUUUUURP**, totally stopping him from saving Bubble O'Gill.

A blast of green lightning exploded from the toilet seat, followed by an ear-splitting

CRRRRFZZZZZZTTTT!!!! as Bubble O'Gill flew through the hole in the seat like a basketball through a hoop.

And then he was gone.

'Uh-oh,' gasped Squidge as the smell of fried fish filled the room.

'What's happening, Squidge?' I asked.

The toilet seat crackled. A thick column of green smoke rose out of it. It spluttered, rattled some more and stopped dead.

'Squidge?' I asked. 'Where is Bubble O'Gill?'

'Not *where*,' said Squidge, peering at the dials on the toilet seat. 'WHEN?'

CHAPTER 8

'So… let me get this straight,' I said after Squidge had explained his historic artefact. 'You built a TIME MACHINE … out of a titanium toilet seat?!'

'Not a time *machine*,' said Squidge. 'A time *squeezer*. Let me explain.'

Squidge scribbled on the whiteboard. He wrote with both hands at once and in less than a minute, the entire board was filled with squiggles and numbers and graphs.

'There!' he said, capping the whiteboard markers. 'Easy-peasy, time-squeezy.'

'Looks like a load of dumb old scientific mumbo jumbo,' said Crichton, stroking his toenail.

'It makes total sense,' said Leanna Kingsley. 'Squidge has created a time window that squeezes all moments in time together in one place. And that window is the hole of the toilet seat. Am I right so far, Squidge?'

'Wholly correct,' smiled Squidge, unrolling some instructions.

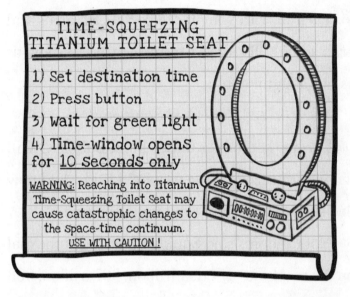

TIME-SQUEEZING
TITANIUM TOILET SEAT

1) Set destination time
2) Press button
3) Wait for green light
4) Time-window opens for <u>10 seconds only</u>

WARNING: Reaching into Titanium Time-Squeezing Toilet Seat may cause catastrophic changes to the space-time continuum.
<u>USE WITH CAUTION!</u>

'So it's kind of like a teeny, tiny time WORMHOLE that opens up for 10 seconds at time. It lets you reach into different times in history,' continued Leanna. 'Only, I'm guessing that you shouldn't go all the way in, or else you'll get SUCKED into another time.'

'Correct!' squeaked Squidge. 'You have to stay in two places at once, or you'll get squeezed into another time.'

'A time squeezer,' I said. 'I get it. That's brilliant, Squidge! And I'm guessing that your plan was to reach in with your SUPER-STRETCHY arms and grab some COOL object from the past to show us as our assignment.'

'Also correct!' squeaked Squidge.

'Except that thanks to Crichton, Bubble O'Gill did get squeezed all the way in,' I said. 'And now he's stuck somewhere random in the past.'

'Not random,' said Squidge, peering at the dial on the machine. '477 quadrillion, 367 trillion, 908 billion, 867 million, 520 thousand, 398 years, 5 months, 23 days, 12 hours, 52 minutes and 48 seconds ago.'

'I never liked Bubble O'Gill anyway,' said Crichton, 'he always smelled fishy.'

TOO BAD.
SO SAD.

'Of course he smelt fishy!' said Abigail Takani. 'He was a FISH!'

'Yeah,' said Daniel Kwon-Yoon. 'And he was OUR fish. We can't leave him stuck back in time. He needs to get back into his tank or else he will be… well, history.'

'We have to find him before Ms Trigley gets back,' I said. 'Or before he causes a big time catastrophe to the entire history of the planet by being the wrong fish at the wrong time.'

'Easy-peasy, time-squeezy,' said Squidge.

'Really?' I said.

'Nup,' said Squidge.

'He's right!' said Leanna Kingsley, holding open Ms Trigley's history book. 'Look!'

CHAPTER 9

It got worse. Bubble O'Gill was on every page of Ms Trigley's history book.

'This is AWESOME!' said Daniel Kwon-Yoon. 'This is a DISASTER!' said Leanna Kingsley. 'Bubble O'Gill has accidentally changed the ENTIRE history of the planet, just by being where – and when – he shouldn't be. Who knows what other problems this has caused?!'

At that moment we became aware of a faint popping sound. Like bubbles bursting.

Then we saw them.

Lenny, Rennie and Shane.

'Whoa!' said Daniel. 'You guys look like Bubble O'Gill!'

Lenny, Rennie and Shane didn't agree. They opened their mouths to protest, but only a popping sound came out.

'Squidge,' I said. 'We have to reach into the titanium time-squeezing toilet seat and grab Bubble O'Gill from the exact moment in time he originally flew through.'

Squidge nodded.

We didn't have much time. Ms Trigley could be back at any second.

'Okay everybody,' I said. 'We have to hold on to Squidge's feet while he stretches through the titanium time-squeezing toilet seat. Squidge will reach through time and try to snatch Bubble

O'Gill back.'

Squidge checked that the toilet seat was set to exactly the same time zone that Bubble O'Gill had been sucked into.

'Be careful, Squidge,' I said as he adjusted the dials.

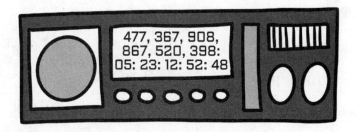

The toilet seat began to hum and vibrate as we waited for the green light to come on.

'Ready Squidge?' I asked.

He gave us the thumbs-up.

'Don't forget, Squidge,' said Leanna. 'You only have 10 seconds to reach in before the time window squeezes shut again.'

The green light clicked on.

'GO!'

CHAPTER 10

Squidge thrust both arms into the toilet seat.

Green sparks crackled through the air. Squidge giggled.

'Can you feel anything?' I asked.

'Uh-huh,' said Squidge, biting his lip. 'Feels…'

'What?'' said Leanne.

'Sloppy,' said Squidge. 'Like a pre-historic plop.'

'Only five seconds left!' I said.

Squidge's arms stretched further and further into the titanium time-squeezing toilet seat.

'Quick Squidge!' I yelled. 'You have to get out!'

'Gnnnnnnnnnnn,' squeaked Squidge, his face turning red.

'Two seconds!' said Leanna.

'Get out, Squidge!' I said.

Squidge whipped his arms backwards.

There was an enormous **PLOP!**

Squidge zipped out of the time squeezer just as it coughed, clattered and shut down.

'Look!' cried Abigail Takani. 'Squidge found Bubble O'Gill!'

Bubble O'Gill was covered in thick, brown mud.

Everyone cheered.

'Oh, yay,' muttered Crichton.

We quickly washed the mud off Bubble O'Gill in the sink.

'He looks kind of... different,' said Abigail, tilting her head sideways.

'Yeah,' said the Pritchard Twin. 'I don't remember him having so many teeth.'

'Or so many eyes,' added Daniel Kwon-Yoon.

'Or so many legs,' I said.

All of a sudden, Bubble O'Gill opened his mouth wide and let out a massive, carnivorous ROAR.

Only it wasn't Bubble O'Gill.

It was this:

'Oops,' squeaked Squidge. 'Wrong fish.'

CHAPTER 11

We had no idea what the creature was. Only that it was fast, angry and **HUNGRY**.

'We have to re-open the time window!' panted Leanna Kingsley as the creature snapped at her legs.

'But I want to keep it as a pet!' said Daniel Kwon-Yoon. 'It's gnarly.'

'And it also wants to **BITE YOUR FACE OFF**,' said the Pritchard Twins.

Squidge meanwhile was resetting the toilet seat.

'Squidge!' I said. 'How long until you can open the time window again?'

'Approximately 43.4965392 seconds,' squeaked Squidge.

'I don't think we're gonna survive that long!' cried Leanna Kingsley as the pre-historic creature snapped at her.

'Maybe it's a vegetarian,' said Daniel Kwon-Yoon, picking up a potted plant and holding it out to the creature.

CRUNCH!

The creature ate the ENTIRE plant, growled angrily and vomited it back out again, all over Crichton.

'Nope,' said Daniel. 'It's definitely not a plant eater.'

'Quick, Squidge!' I said as the creature sped after us again.

'Ten seconds,' squeaked Squidge. The machine hummed and rattled.

'How are we even going to get it through the time window?' I asked.

'Throw Crichton through first as bait,' suggested the Pritchard Twins.

Bait. I thought. *I know what to do…*

'Seven seconds,' squeaked Squidge.

'**OWWW!**' cried Crichton. 'It bit my hair!'

'Three seconds,' squeaked Squidge.

'Here, freaky, carnivorous, prehistoric eating machine!' I called, holding up my lunchbox. 'Padman's got an extra-tasty, frozen beef curry for you.'

I opened the lid. It was one of my dad's extra-strong recipes. Three parts stewed beef, five parts onion, 10 parts hot chilli. And it was still frozen solid.

'Time!' squeaked Squidge.

The green light flicked on. Sparks flew out of the toilet seat. I threw the frozen block of curry towards the creature.

As it leapt up and caught the frozen curry block it howled in outrage and got stuck in the toilet seat.

'Got it!' yelled Abigail Takani.

The creature burst back up out of the toilet seat, jaws snapping.

'We don't got it,' said Abigail.

'Sit!' squeaked Squidge, jumping straight in front of the creature. It howled ferociously and snapped it jaws open so wide that you could see the inside of its stomach. 'I said SIT!' squeaked Squidge, inflating himself to the size of a car and growling at the creature.

The creature growled back even louder, big stringy gloops of saliva dripping from its jaws.

Squidge didn't budge. He kept staring straight onto the creature's eyes so that it didn't notice him stretching an arm around the back of the toilet seat and flicking a switch.

The machine grinded like a chainsaw. The creature wailed in outrage and was sucked into it.

Sparks crackled from the toilet seat, followed by a **HUGE** spray of sticky lime-coloured gloop. It burst out like an explosion of fluorescent diarrhoea.

None of it missed Crichton.

'Ugh!' groaned everyone. '**THAT STINKS!**'

'Squidge,' I said. 'What did you do to it?'

Squidge giggled.

'Full flush mode.'

CHAPTER 12

Squidge reset the toilet seat and we tried again.

'You can do it, Squidge,' said Abigail Takani as we waited for the green light. 'Wherever Bubble O'Gill is trapped, we'll find him!'

'Or *when*ever he is trapped,' added Leanna Kingsley.

'Just try not to think about the fact that Bubble O'Gill could be taking his last, crispy breaths in some burning, pre-historic desert,' added Daniel Kwon-Yoon.

'Or that you only have 10 seconds to reach through the toilet seat,' added Abigail.

'Or that Lenny, Rennie and Shane could be stuck as human-puffer-fish forever,' said Daniel.

'That's not really helping,' said Leanna.

The green light on the titanium time-squeezing toilet seat lit up again.

Squidge plunged his arms in.

Three seconds later, he pulled them out again.

'AAAAAAAAAUGH!' said Shane Sloosman. 'VIKING!'

Sure enough, Squidge had pulled out a Viking. She was holding a GIANT, SPIKY mace that Squidge had mistaken for Bubble O'Gill.

'I think I'm in love!' said Daniel Kwon-Yoon.

'I think we're in trouble,' I said.

Another Viking was poking his head out of the time squeezer.

He shouted something nonsensical.

Lenny, Rennie and Shane tried to scream, but it sounded like bubble wrap being popped.

'He says his name is Blarkoff the Beheader and he's asking who stole his beloved fiancée Astrid the Annihilator,' said the Pritchard twins.

'How do you know what he's saying?' I whispered.

'We speak Viking,' said the Pritchard Twins, shrugging. 'Learned it on YouTube.'

The second Viking leaped out of the toilet seat. He was tiny. Even smaller than Squidge.

Now Astrid the Annihilator started yabbering at Blarkoff the Beheader.

'She says that she is *not* his fiancée,' whispered the Pritchard Twins. 'And that she is not interested in being stuck at home cooking his dinner and having his babies.'

'I like her,' whispered Abigail Takani, as Blarkoff the Beheader stomped his feet and argued with Astrid.

'Now he says that he'll do anything for her and just wants her to follow her dreams and be happy,' whispered the Pritchard Twins.

'Aww, how romantic,' whispered Abigail as Blarkoff knelt on one knee in front of Astrid.

'Now she's saying that if he agrees to an equal share of all domestic duties and that they alternate who gets to go on Viking raids, she *might* consider his marriage proposal,' whispered the Pritchard Twins.

Everyone was quiet as Blarkoff scratched his

beard and considered Astrid's terms. Finally he placed his sword at her feet and nodded.

'He agrees!' said the Pritchard Twins.

Everyone cheered.

Rebecca Peterson pulled out her trumpet and started playing the wedding march.

The two Vikings hugged each other.

'AWWW,' we said.

The two Vikings started kissing each other.

'EWWWWWW,' we groaned.

Then Squidge crept up behind them with the toilet seat and switched it on. The Vikings were sucked into it with a CRACKLE and a ZAP.

'Those were some nutty Vikings,' said Daniel Kwon-Yoon. 'History is actually pretty entertaining.'

A series of metallic **CLANGS** echoed across the room.

The Pritchard twins were battling each other with the Vikings' swords.

'They left them behind,' they said, shrugging. 'Somebody needs to look after them.'

They leapt into battle again and everyone gathered around to watch.

'Guys!' I said. 'Aren't you forgetting something?'

Everyone stopped and looked at me.

'Bubble O'Gill?'

I turned to Squidge.

'Fire up the toilet seat, Dibs,' I said. 'Time to go TIME-FISHING.'

CHAPTER 13

Time was running out. Lenny, Rennie and Shane were drying out.

Squidge's next search in the titanium time-squeezing toilet seat produced a baby brontosaurus, closely followed by a pteranodon.

Rennie desperately wanted to keep them so they could be friends with his pet python, but Leanna explained that we were in serious danger of messing up the space-time continuum even more than we already had.

'We have to hurry!' I said 'Ms Trigley could be back any minute. And whenever in time he is, Bubble O'Gill might not even be able to breathe.'

'Poor Bubble O'Gill,' said Abigail Takani, wiping back a tear. 'I hope he landed in a nice friendly pond somewhere.'

'Forget about Bubble O'Dill,' said Crichton. 'Fact is, that dumb fish has been dead for millions of years now. Maybe we can find his fossil and make a nice little tombstone for him.'

Squidge glared at Crichton. Then he started to grow.

'I was just kidding,' Crichton gulped. He edged backwards, treading on the baby brontosaurus's tail.

It yelped and bit him on the butt.

'Looks like brontosauruses were meat eaters after all,' chuckled Abigail Takani.

Crichton yelped and accidentally knocked the titanium time-squeezing toilet seat off the table.

'**NOOOOO!!!**' I yelled.

But it was too late. The toilet seat hit the carpet with a CRUNCH.

Green sparks filled the room.

There was an ominous rumbling.

Black smoke billowed from the toilet seat.

'Not good,' said Squidge.

There was a bright orange EXPLOSION. An enormous river of red molten gloops, sprayed across the floor.

'Look out!' I said, leaping up onto a desk. 'The floor is LAVA!'

CHAPTER 14

The funny thing about lava is that it is hot, molten and MELTS THINGS.

We jumped up on our desks, which immediately started to melt.

The pteranodon smashed through the window and flew away, squawking.

The baby brontosaurus bounded out the door and disappeared down the corridor.

'Nice work, Cry-bum!' said Leanna Kingsley, dangling from the ceiling fan.

'Wasn't my fault!' screeched Crichton, desperately trying not to topple off his melting desk.

'Is it hot in here, or what?' said Daniel Kwon-Yoon, hanging from the overhead light.

The carpet started to cook.

'The lava is eating through the floor!' cried Leanna.

There was an angry yelp from the classroom below.

'Wait a minute...' I said. 'Wasn't Janitor Hoovesly painting the classroom underneath ours today?'

'He was,' said Daniel, peering out the window. 'Now he's screaming across the playground covered in molten lava.'

Much as we all loved the idea of our old arch-nemesis being barbequed, we knew that we were in the middle of a catastrophic time catastrophe of catastrophic proportions.

Luckily Squidge was on the case.

While we'd been escaping the lava, Squidge had grabbed the titanium time-squeezing toilet seat and reset it.

There was another blinding flash of green light as Squidge thrust his arms through once again.

At the same moment, the whole building started to SHAKE.

The walls started to CRUMBLE.

The heat from the lava was overpowering.

'Come on, Squidge!' I urged. The legs of my desk were entirely melted and there was only a thin piece of wood between my feet and the lava.

Squidge stretched his torso through the titanium time-squeezing toilet seat.

'GNNNNNNNNNNN!!!!' he yelled.

'BE CAREFUL, SQUIDGE!' I said.

But he was stretching further and further through the toilet set. Only his feet were sticking out now.

'He's been in there for 8 seconds!' said Leanna.

'SQUIDGE!!!!' I said, as the walls of the classroom began to crack and crumble. 'Pull out!'

There was an enormous ZZZZZNNNNNTTTT sound followed by a crunchy, cranking CLUNK.

Then the WEIRDEST THING HAPPENED.

CHAPTER 15

Hundreds of Squidge Dibleys appeared from nowhere.

Only, not all of him. Just his front half, looped and looped in a **MASSIVE** cobweb of knots.

'Whhhooooooaaa!' said Daniel Kwon-Yoon. 'This is so freaky!'

All the Squidges closed their eyes and squeezed themselves into a tight knot. For a moment, everything looked like it was becoming jelly. A **SQUELCHY** sound echoed from everywhere.

At that moment, the lava began sucking back

through the titanium time-squeezing toilet seat. It was like the toilet seat had turned into an ultra-powered vacuum cleaner.

The walls of the classroom started to reassemble. The floor connected back together. Everything started moving backwards

My brain felt like it was on rewind. My breath started going in reverse.

Everyone started talking in reverse, which is why I didn't understand a word of what Leanne Kingsley said:

SQUIDGE IS A GENIUS! HE HAS LOOPED HIMSELF THROUGH THE TIME-SQUEEZER TO TIE THE TIME BACK TOGETHER AGAIN!

It turned out that Squidge was literally tying himself in a giant time knot, to tie time back together again.

The baby brontosaurus galloped backwards into the classroom and was SUCKED through the toilet seat. It was immediately followed the pteranodon flying in reverse and unsmashing the classroom window as it too was SWALLOWED into the toilet seat.

Outside, Janitor Hoovesly sprinted backwards into the classroom below.

'It's working!' cried Leanna Kingsley, backwards. 'Squidge is tying time back together again!'

The building shook.

The last gloops of lava disappeared into the toilet seat.

Our melted desks grew legs again.

The carpet repaired itself.

Lenny, Rennie and Shane's fishy spikes disappeared.

Then, with a rushing, reeling, spinning **SWOOSH** all the loops of Squidges flew backwards into nothingness until all that was left were his feet sticking out of the titanium time-squeezing toilet seat.

His body shuddered.

The seat vibrated.

Green smoke billowed from the seat.

Then, Squidge's voice echoed from somewhere in the distance. It was as if it was coming from everywhere and nowhere at once. It said:

'ꓢTUUUUUUUUUUUUUUUUUUUUUUUUUUUUUUUUUUUU UUUUUUUUUUUUUUUUUUUUUUUUUUUUUUUUUUUUUUU UUUUUUUUUUUUUUUUUUUUUUUUUUUUUUUUUUUUUUU UUUUUUUUUUUUUUUUUUUUUUUUUUUUUUUUUUUUUUU UUUUUUUUUUUUUUUUUUUUUUUUUUUUUUUUUUUUUUU UUUUUUUUUUUUUUUUUUCK!!!'

'What did he say?' said Abigail Takani.

'Sounded like shmuck…' said Daniel Kwon-Yoon, uncertainly.

'Or cluck…?' said Leanna Kingsley.

'Duck, maybe?' said the Pritchard Twins.

Squidge's voice echoed again, longer and more desperate this time.

'STUUUUUUUUUUUUUUUUUUUUUUUUUUUUUUUUUUUU
UUUUUUUUUUUUUUUUUUUUUUUUUUUUUUUUUUUUUUUU
UUUUUUUUUUUUUUUUUUUUUUUUUUUUUUUUUUUUUUUU
UUUUUUUUUUUUUUUUUUUUUUUUUUUUUUUUUUUUUUUU
UUUUUUUUUUUUUUUUUUUUUUUUUUUUUUUUUUUUUUUU
UUUUUUUUUUUUUUUUUUUUUUUUUUUUUUUUUUCK!!!'

'STUCK!' I said. 'He's stuck in time! We need to pull him out! Quick, everybody!'

We grabbed Squidge's feet and pulled him backwards as hard as we could.

83

'He's slipping!' yelled Leanna.

We pulled harder.

'He's stretching!' yelled Abigail.

We pulled with all our might. But it was like we were trying to drag the past back into the present.

Finally, with an enormous

POP!

Squidge burst out of the titanium time-squeezing toilet seat.

His glasses were hanging off.

His eyes were crossed.

He was inflated like a massive balloon.

But there, held tightly in his arms, was Bubble O'Gill.

'Easy peasy time-squeezy,' squeaked Squidge.

CHAPTER 16

'Hope you kids haven't been bored while I was out,' said Ms Trigley as she walked back into the classroom. 'I had to help Principal Shoutmouth remove a kindergartener's head from their lunchbox.'

She sniffed the air.

'Has someone been cooking fish?' she asked, looking around the room.

We all blinked innocently, even Bubble O'Gill who was happily back in his bowl.

'Well, actually,' said Crichton Peel, standing up. 'While you were out –'

'UGGHH!!!'

Crichton gagged as Abigail Takani jammed her pencil case in his mouth.

Ms Trigley regarded Crichton for a moment.

'Crichton,' she said. 'How many times have I asked you not to eat other students' stationery?'

'BBBTTT I NNNNDD TTTT TLLL YYYSMMMTHNGG!!' protested Crichton, trying to get the pencil case out of his gob.

'That'll do Crichton,' said Ms Trigley. 'You had your turn already.'

Like I've said before, Ms Trigley is an AWESOME teacher. I guess she'd figured that whatever we'd been up to was best left unsaid. And she certainly didn't want to hear it from Crichton.

'So,' she continued. 'Squidge, would you like

to show us what your toilet seat can do?'

Everyone looked at Squidge.

He rubbed his chin.

'Maybe another time?' he squeaked.

Which would have been the end of it, had Crichton not spat the pencil case out of his mouth, and leapt at the toilet seat, shouting,

'MS TRIGLEY! THIS TOILET SEAT IS ACTUALLY A TI-'

Too bad Crichton forgot that you should never shout near Squidge.

It sets off his Nervous Belly Belchus.

Which is why Ms Trigley never heard Crichton say 'TIME MACHINE'.

Squidge's BUUUUUUURP drowned out all other noise.

It was SO LOUD, the sound waves blasted Crichton into the air.

He **BOUNCED** off the ceiling and landed right on top of Squidge.

Squidge instantly inflated, on account of his marshmallow muscles and bungee bones, which sent Crichton flying upwards again. He rebounded off the ceiling fan and landed right on the titanium time-squeezing toilet seat.

Well, his butt landed right in the titanium toilet seat.

A blast of green lightning exploded across the room, followed by an ear splitting

CRRRRFZZZZZZTTTT!!!!

Which is how Squidge won the genuine, limited edition Dr Doogles mega-jumbo-sized Golden Chocolate egg and Crichton's butt accidently ended up making history.

But that's a story for another time.

Besides, Squidge and I have an egg to eat.

About MICK ELLIOTT

At school, Mick Elliott got into HEAPS of trouble for drawing disgusting pictures in class. Now he gets to write and draw hilarious stories as a real job (which makes up for the fact that he's all old and wrinkly).

For most of his grown-up life, Mick worked as a TV producer at Nickelodeon, creating hit shows like *Slime Cup, Camp Orange, SlimeFest* and the *Kids' Choice Awards*.

His first book series, The Turners, was nominated for an Aurealis Award and features on the Premier's Reading Challenge.

Mick loves visiting schools to talk about creative writing, illustrating and what to do when you accidentally fart in class.

Check out other books by Mick Elliott:

www.mickelliott.me

@whatmicksaw on Instagram

HOW TO DRAW
SQUIDGE DIBLEY !

Don't worry if your first
attempts are a bit wonky.

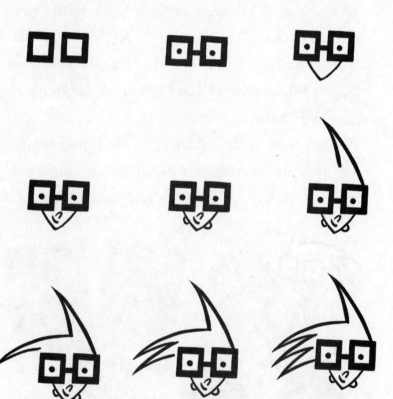

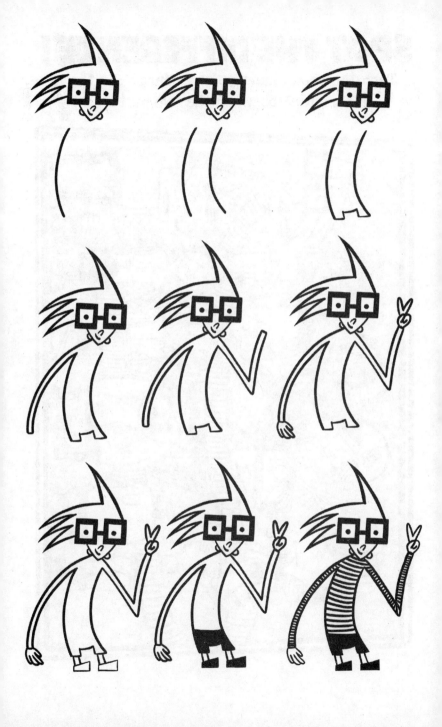

SPOT THE DIFFERENCE !

Turn the book sideways and search for the 12 differences between the two pictures !